I FEEL FIVE!

Bethanie Deeney Murguia

CANDLEWICK PRESS

First edition 2014

Library of Congress Catalog Card Number 2013952832
ISBN 978-0-7636-6291-2

CCP 19 18 17 16 15 14
10 9 8 7 6 5 4 3 2 1

Printed in Shenzhen, Guangdong, China

This book was typeset in Caecilia Roman.
The illustrations were done in pen and ink and watercolor.

Candlewick Press
99 Dover Street
Somerville, Massachusetts 02144

visit us at www.candlewick.com

For my nephew Super Jack

On his fourth birthday, Fritz Newton ate
birthday pancakes, got his very own cape,
and picked apples for birthday pie.

Being four was fun, but tomorrow . . .

Fritz will be five! And he is quite sure that five will feel very different. He'll probably even lose his first tooth.

First thing, Fritz checks his teeth. Not even a wiggle.
He stares into the mirror. Everything *looks* the same.

Everything *feels* the same, too.

"Happy birthday, Fritz!" says Mama
   at breakfast.

"It's your big day," says Papa.

Fritz eats his birthday pancakes—
all five of them—but he still feels four.

Before he leaves for school, Fritz opens his present—
new sneakers that fit perfectly.

"They match my cape!" Fritz exclaims.

Bounce,

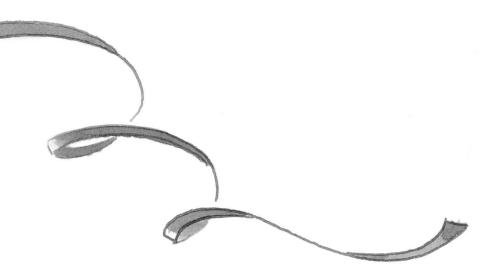

ZOOOOOoom,

flip!

But when he can't tie his shoelaces,
Fritz feels four again.

I'll feel five when I'm the birthday king at school, he thinks.

"Happy birthday, Fritz!" says Miss Macaroon.
"How does it feel to be five?"

"So far, five feels a lot like four," he says.

Everyone sings as Miss Macaroon places
the birthday crown on his head.

During the song, Fritz thinks, *five, five, five, five, five.*

But nothing changes.

After school, Fritz realizes that he still
can't whistle, snap his fingers . . .

or do the monkey bars
two at a time.

Plus he can still count all his years
on one hand—the same as before.

Then he hears a quiet voice say, "Excuse me,
I think you dropped your cape."

Fritz looks up.

"Can you reach the apples?" the girl asks.

Fritz thinks for a minute.

Then he bounces. He zooms. He soars.

He plucks two perfect apples.

Fritz feels a little different now;
maybe a *little* more five.

And when he takes a bite . . .

Fritz is quite sure that one of his
teeth wiggles, just a bit.